Little Stowaway

for Michael Philip Johnston T.T.

The publishers and author are indebted to the Sutcliffe Gallery, Whitby
for permission to reproduce the photograph of John Robert and to Dora Walker's
Freemen of the Sea (A. Brown & Son 1951) for details of his life.

A Red Fox Book

Published by Random House Children's Books
20 Vauxhall Bridge Road, London SW1V 2SA
A division of Random House UK Ltd
London Melbourne Sydney Auckland
Johannesburg and agencies throughout the world

1 3 5 7 9 10 8 6 4 2

First published in Great Britain by Julia MacRae 1997

Red Fox edition 1999

Printed in Hong Kong by Midas Printing Limited

RANDOM HOUSE UK Limited Reg. No. 954009

ISBN 0 09 960571 6

Little Stowaway

Theresa Tomlinson
& Jane Browne

RED FOX

Tom Dryden was a fisherman. He worked on a trawler that steamed through the cold North Sea to the great fishing grounds of the Dogger Bank.

Cod, haddock, mackerel, whiting!

It was a happy time for his family when Tom came home with a ship full of fish; it meant money for food and sometimes for new clothes. But each time Tom set off to sea, his wife and children felt sad.

John Robert, the youngest child, loved his father dearly. He also loved the great smoky fish-smelling boat *North Star* where his father worked. He longed to go to sea in her.

One October day, John Robert followed his father down to the harbour. While Tom Dryden stowed his baggage under his bunk in *North Star*, John Robert slipped up the plank. In the noise and bustle of departure nobody noticed him. He scrambled down the ladder into the ship's hold and hid behind the coal box.

A shout went up, "Cast her off! C..a..st her off!"
With excitement John Robert heard the screw thresh the
water as the great trawler chugged away from the docks,
heading out into the grey water of the North Sea.

The fishermen ate their supper and climbed into their
bunks to sleep. Only the skipper and his mate were awake
in the wheelhouse.

Behind the coal box it was dark and lonely and John Robert began to feel very sick. As the ship rolled through the waves, his stomach went up and down. At last he was so tired he fell asleep.

Next day, John Robert no longer felt sick but he was numb with cold. Still he dare not call out. He was afraid of Tom Dryden's anger when he found his son on board *North Star*. Now he felt very hungry. The delicious smell of fried fish and freshly boiled plum duff came wafting down to the hold, making his mouth water. Late that night, the little boy heard a scratching sound. Bright eyes glistened in the darkness. "Rats!" he tried to scream, but he was so frightened and cold and hungry that no sound came. He fainted right away.

Early next morning the ship's cook came down into the hold. He filled his bucket with coal and started to climb back up the ladder. Suddenly he stopped!

"Is that a foot?" he said. "A dirty little foot?" He put down his bucket and went to look behind the coal box. He couldn't believe his eyes. "Fetch Tom Dryden," he shouted, "fetch him quick! Tell him I've found a little rat at the back of the coal box!"

His shouts brought the men clambering down into the hold.

"A stowaway! We've got a stowaway!"

Even the skipper came to see what they'd found. "Bring blankets," he shouted. "And warm up some broth!"

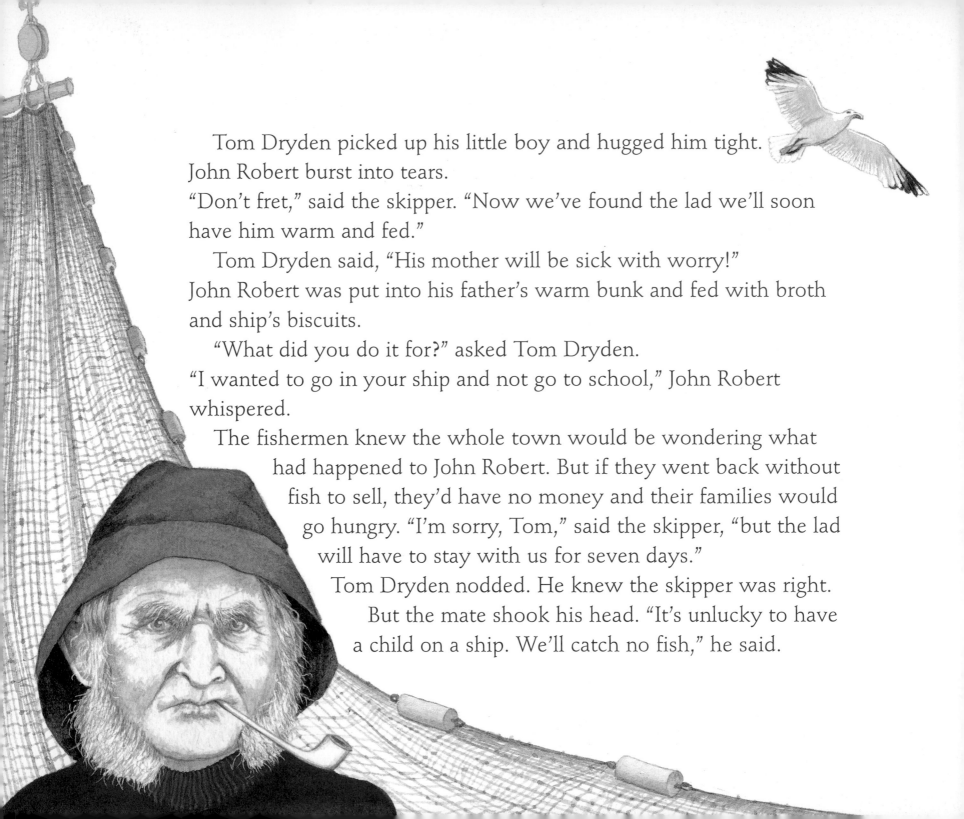

Tom Dryden picked up his little boy and hugged him tight. John Robert burst into tears.

"Don't fret," said the skipper. "Now we've found the lad we'll soon have him warm and fed."

Tom Dryden said, "His mother will be sick with worry!" John Robert was put into his father's warm bunk and fed with broth and ship's biscuits.

"What did you do it for?" asked Tom Dryden.

"I wanted to go in your ship and not go to school," John Robert whispered.

The fishermen knew the whole town would be wondering what had happened to John Robert. But if they went back without fish to sell, they'd have no money and their families would go hungry. "I'm sorry, Tom," said the skipper, "but the lad will have to stay with us for seven days."

Tom Dryden nodded. He knew the skipper was right. But the mate shook his head. "It's unlucky to have a child on a ship. We'll catch no fish," he said.

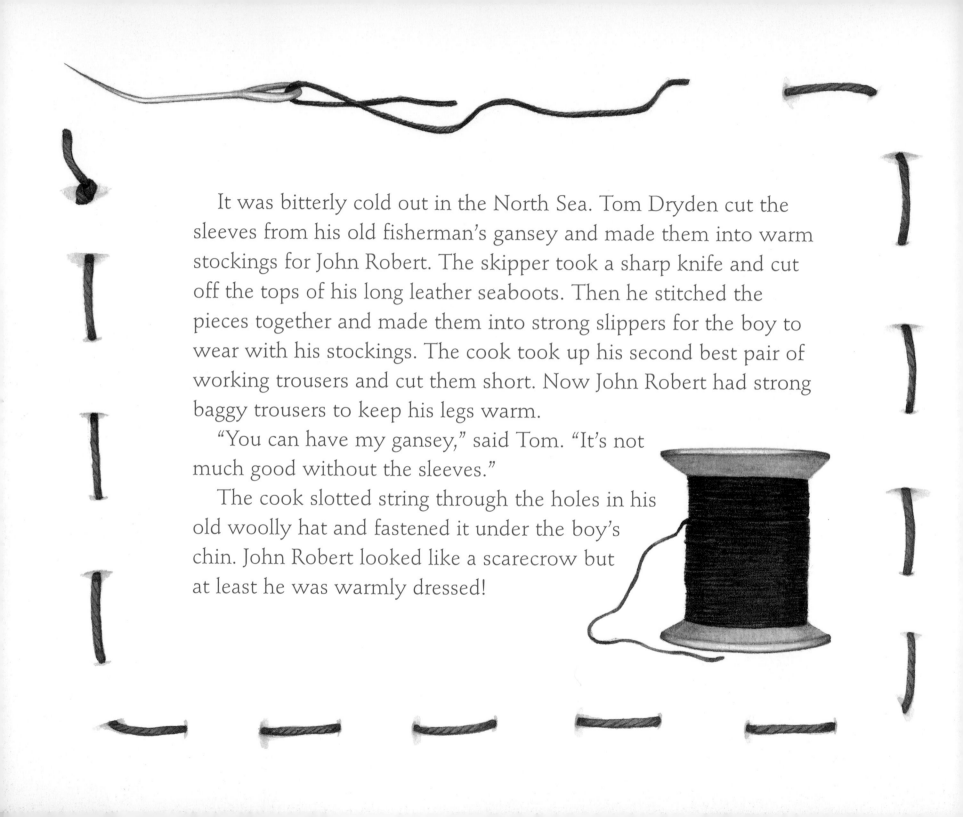

It was bitterly cold out in the North Sea. Tom Dryden cut the sleeves from his old fisherman's gansey and made them into warm stockings for John Robert. The skipper took a sharp knife and cut off the tops of his long leather seaboots. Then he stitched the pieces together and made them into strong slippers for the boy to wear with his stockings. The cook took up his second best pair of working trousers and cut them short. Now John Robert had strong baggy trousers to keep his legs warm.

"You can have my gansey," said Tom. "It's not much good without the sleeves."

The cook slotted string through the holes in his old woolly hat and fastened it under the boy's chin. John Robert looked like a scarecrow but at least he was warmly dressed!

That night, as they fished in the cold and the silence of the darkness, the crew sat on deck and sang hymns and songs about catching fish.

North Star, North Star, Guide us where we roam,

Fill our net with fine fat fish Then take us safely home.

In the morning when they pulled in their nets, they couldn't believe their eyes. Thousands of fish flapped and flopped into the big box on the deck. They flew up in the air and slid down the collars and sleeves of the fishermen, there were so many of them! Covered in fish scales, John Robert leapt up and down and clapped his hands in delight.

A basket for cod, a basket for haddock, a basket for mackerel, a basket for whiting. The men worked hard, sorting their catch and John Robert helped them. Then they gutted their fish.

"Watch out!" shouted Tom. A sharp-toothed cat-fish wriggled and snapped at John Robert's ankle. The skipper snatched it up by its tail and flung it safely into the biggest basket.

It was the largest catch they had ever made. "You've brought us luck, John Robert," said the skipper. "Now we can turn back home." They called John Robert the mascot of the *North Star*. He had never been so happy.

North Star docked in the middle of the night. Tom Dryden strode up the path from the harbour with John Robert riding on his shoulders. Just as dawn was breaking he knocked on the cottage door.

"Open up, Mother!" he called. "See what a fine fish I've brought you."

John Robert's mother drew back the bedroom curtains, and saw her son. She flung open the window and stretched out her arms. Tears of happiness rolled down her cheeks as she lifted him up from his father's shoulders and pulled him inside.

Tom Dryden waited on his doorstep but nobody came to greet him. John Robert's mother was so pleased to see her child safe that she had forgotten her husband!

Tom knocked loud and long and shouted, "I never took him on purpose, Mother!"

Then at last all the family came downstairs. They flung open
the door, laughing and crying with joy. "Come in, Father," they said.
"Welcome home!"

This is based on a true story of the North-East coast. The baby in the basket is John Robert who, at the age of twelve, was awarded a medal for rescuing a man from drowning. Later he became a lifeboat man.

Some bestselling Red Fox picture books

THE BIG ALFIE AND ANNIE ROSE STORYBOOK
by Shirley Hughes
OLD BEAR
by Jane Hissey
OI! GET OFF OUR TRAIN
by John Burningham
DON'T DO THAT!
by Tony Ross
NOT NOW, BERNARD
by David McKee
ALL JOIN IN
by Quentin Blake
THE WHALES' SONG
by Gary Blythe and Dyan Sheldon
JESUS' CHRISTMAS PARTY
by Nicholas Allan
THE PATCHWORK CAT
by Nicola Bayley and William Mayne
WILLY AND HUGH
by Anthony Browne
THE WINTER HEDGEHOG
by Ann and Reg Cartwright
A DARK, DARK TALE
by Ruth Brown
HARRY, THE DIRTY DOG
by Gene Zion and Margaret Bloy Graham
DR XARGLE'S BOOK OF EARTHLETS
by Jeanne Willis and Tony Ross
WHERE'S THE BABY?
by Pat Hutchins